Beast Quest

C ct the special coins in this book.
You will earn one gold coin for
every chapter you read.

Once you have finished all the chapters,
find out what to do with your gold coins at
the back of the book.

With special thanks to Tabitha Jones

For Harrison J. O. Smith

www.beastquest.co.uk

ORCHARD BOOKS
Carmelite House
50 Victoria Embankment
London EC4Y 0DZ

A Paperback Original
First published in Great Britain in 2015

Beast Quest is a registered trademark of Beast Quest Limited
Series created by Beast Quest Limited, London

Text © Beast Quest Limited 2015
Cover and inside illustrations by Steve Sims
© Beast Quest Limited 2015

A CIP catalogue record for this book is available from
the British Library.

ISBN 978 1 40833 986 2

1 3 5 7 9 10 8 6 4 2

Printed in Great Britain

MIX
Paper from
responsible sources
FSC® C104740

The paper and board used in this book are made from wood
from responsible sources.

Orchard Books
An imprint of Hachette Children's Group
Part of The Watts Publishing Group Limited
An Hachette UK company

www.hachette.co.uk

STYRO
THE SNAPPING BRUTE

BY ADAM BLADE

ORCHARD

CONTENTS

Greetings, followers of the Quest,

I am Irina, the Good Witch of Avantia's twin kingdom, Gwildor. This was supposed to be a time of happiness, as we welcomed young heroes Tom and Elenna to our capital city Jengtor. Freya, Tom's mother and Mistress of the Beasts, beamed with pride at the thought of her son's arrival.

She smiles no longer.

Someone else has been awaiting Tom's arrival. We should have known our enemies would choose this moment to strike. Now Freya lies in my chamber, unable to command her Beasts. And Jengtor is under siege from a deadly menace that attacks from the skies.

Our only hope lies with Tom and Elenna, but they are walking right into a trap.

Irina, loyal Witch of Gwildor

AN UNEXPECTED WELCOME

Tom leaned from the prow of the boat, excitement building inside him. He was heading back to his mother's homeland for the first time in ages, and he was really looking forward to the visit. Fresh, salty air swept past his face and the approaching shoreline shone with a fierce, trembling brightness only possible in the kingdom of Gwildor. Ahead, white-capped waves lapped at a narrow stretch of sandy beach giving way to emerald grassland, then lush, forested hills. Tom lifted a hand to shield his eyes from the brilliant, jewel-like colours, and squinted towards a wooden dock

that stretched from the beach into the sea.

"Almost there!" Elenna said from beside him. "And it looks like we're going to travel to Jengtor in style!"

A gilded coach stood at the end of the jetty. It was harnessed to a pair of dappled grey horses, with a stout coachman seated at the front.

As Tom's eyes adjusted to the intense colours, he saw that the door of the coach was decorated with Gwildor's imperial seal – a green dragon flying over snowy clouds. But there was no sign of his mother, Freya. Tom's excitement faded, and a twinge of worry took its place.

"I was looking forward to spending time with my mother on the ride to Jengtor," he said. "I wonder why she's changed her plans."

"I hope it's nothing serious," Elenna said, peering towards the coach. "But I suppose we'll find out soon enough. With a coach like that, we should reach the capital in no time."

As their ship cut through the surf towards the jetty, Tom pulled on the tiller, turning them into the wind. The sails started to flap, and the vessel slowed. As soon as they were close enough, Tom steered parallel to the wooden quay, bringing them gently into dock. Seabirds wheeled overhead, screeching and squabbling; the sun beat down fiercely, making the air around them shimmer with heat. Elenna leapt from the prow onto the wooden boards of the quay, and fastened them to a mooring. Tom jumped down beside her, and they headed inland.

The brawny coachman stepped

down from his seat, and raised
a hand as they approached.
"Greetings," he said, gruffly. Tom
felt stifled just looking at the man's
long, heavy cloak and leather boots.
A thick black beard covered his
chin and neck.

*I suppose he must be used to this
heat!* Tom thought.

The man opened the coach door,
and bowed low to Tom and Elenna,
gesturing with his hand that they
should climb inside. "Freya sends
her apologies," he said, his head still
bowed. "But Angel and Star are the
fastest horses in Gwildor. We will
carry you to her swiftly."

"Thank you," Elenna said,

stepping into the coach and
settling herself on a padded velvet
bench. Tom sat beside her, and the
coachman closed the door with a
clunk. A moment later, Tom heard
the scrape of boots on wood as the
man took his seat.

"Walk on!" he called to his horses. The coach lurched and veered sharply right with a jolt that threw Tom against Elenna.

There was the sharp crack of a whip, and the horses whinnied. The coach swerved back to the left, and the coachman muttered an angry oath under his breath.

Elenna raised her eyebrows. "Someone's having a bad day," she said. "Maybe the horses are newly trained?"

Tom frowned. "Or maybe the coachman is? Certainly he needs to learn better manners."

Elenna settled back into her seat. "Well, even if the ride is a bit bumpy, we should try to relax. There won't be much time to rest when we reach Jengtor, what with all the visiting and sightseeing we've got planned."

Tom nodded and leaned back beside his friend, relaxing into the soft cushioned seat. Sailing was heavy work, and his shoulders ached from their long voyage. Before long, he found himself slipping into a daydream as he listened to the steady clip-clop of the horses' hooves. *I wonder if Freya will have prepared a feast...* he thought. It had been a long time since he'd tasted Gwildorian food, and his mouth ater at the thought.

es lapped at the beach
with a gentle shushing
sound. It should have been
soothing, but somehow it made Tom
feel uneasy. *Something isn't right...*
With a jolt of alarm, Tom realised
what. The sea was on his left. *We're
going the wrong way!*

Tom poked his head though the
window and called to the coachman
above. "Why are we following the
coast road south?" he asked. "We
need to turn inland if we want to
reach Jengtor."

"Aye," the coachman said. "And
I'll be heading west shortly. The
road I'll take is smoother, and we'll

make better time."

Tom frowned. *What road?* He turned back to Elenna, and saw that her lips were pinched together with worry.

"That doesn't sound right to me," she said.

Tom put his hand to the yellow jewel in his shield, using its magic to remember the map of Gwildor.

"It isn't right," he said. "If we keep going this way, and then head west, we'll end up in the Rainbow Jungle." Tom leant back through the window.

"How far to the road?" he asked.

"It's just up yonder," the coachman said, lifting a hand to

point. His sleeve fell back, revealing
a hairy, muscled forearm and
the edge of a blue-black stain. *A
tattoo?* Tom's stomach clenched

as he noticed the jagged teeth of a reptilian skull at the base of the mark – the mark of the Pirate King, Sanpao. Tom ducked back into the carriage, his pulse racing. *He's a pirate!*

"Tom!" Elenna clutched his arm and pointed through her window out to sea. A bulky shape was sailing towards them across the sky, casting a dark shadow onto the waves below. It had a curved hull and billowing sails, and at the top of its foremast, a Beast-skull flag fluttered in the wind.

Sanpao's flying ship!

AMBUSH FROM THE SKY

Tom's heart thudded in his chest as the coach jolted onwards, carrying them straight into Sanpao's trap. *How could I have been so stupid?* He swallowed the fear rising in his throat and stood up straight, the carriage rocking beneath him. *I have to act now with surprise on my side!*

Elenna tugged her bow from her back. "What's the plan?" she said.

"You stay here," Tom said. "Keep an eye on Sanpao's ship. I'm going to take control of this coach." He hopped onto the bench, reached his

arms through the window to grab
the roof and pulled himself out. The
coachman was hunched forwards,
perched on the edge of his seat. Tom
heaved himself up onto the roof
and steadied himself against the

swaying. As he bent his knees, ready to lunge towards the pirate's back, the man turned, and let out a harsh bark of laughter.

"Too late for that, boy," he said, flicking the reins. Tom's feet shot out from under him and he tumbled backwards.

SMACK! The air was punched out of his lungs as he landed on the ground. Tom scrambled to his feet, his shoulder throbbing with pain.

The coach rumbled away, churning up a trail of dust. Tom harnessed the power of his golden leg armour to increase his speed as he raced after it. The coach driver lifted his whip and brought it down

with a savage crack, driving the
horses onward.

Ahead, Sanpao's flying ship
hovered over the beach, long ropes
uncoiling from its gunwale to the
ground. It was close enough that
Tom could see the glint of the
pirates' weapons. Their vicious
laughter reached his ears.

Tom shifted his attention back
to the coach. Elenna was leaning
out of the window, an arrow aimed
upwards at the ship. Her bow
swung wildly with every jolt of the
carriage.

I have to help her! Tom thought.
He called on the power of his golden
leg armour and sprinted onwards.

Already, the first pirates were shimmying down the trailing ropes towards the beach.

"Come on, you puny maggots!" one lank-haired pirate shouted, pausing in his climb to wave his cutlass at Tom.

"You snot-nosed ragamuffins don't stand a chance!" another cried.

Elenna let her arrow fly towards the pirates, but it fell harmlessly into the sand. She pulled her head back into the carriage. Tom raced on, gaining steadily on the coach. When he finally judged he was close enough, he focussed on the right-hand mare. Then he called on the power of his golden boots, and leapt. His legs wheeled in the air as he flew over the coach and driver...

Thud! He landed in the horse's saddle and grabbed the reins. The

mare whinnied and reared up, but Tom held the reins steady, bringing the frightened creature's hooves clattering back to earth.

He leaned close to the horse's ear. "Be calm, friend," he said, then sat back in the saddle and tugged the reins. "Whoa!" he cried. Both horses responded at once, thundering to a stop.

SCREECH! Tom glanced back to see the carriage lurch. The coachman was thrown forwards, landing face-first in the sand. There was a hideous crack as the wooden hitching connecting the horses to the coach snapped. The coach tipped, teetering on two wheels.

No! Tom watched in horror as the coach crashed down onto its side. *Elenna could be badly injured!*

But he couldn't help her now.

The pirate coachman was storming towards him, his face purple with rage as he spat sand from his lips.

Tom swung from his horse's back, tugging his sword from his belt and striding to meet the pirate. The bearded man threw off his cloak, revealing stained leathers and muscled arms covered with Beast tattoos. He drew his cutlass and charged. Tom waited until the man was almost on him, then he brought his own blade whistling down.

CLANG! He knocked the cutlass clean from the pirate's grip.
The man snarled and turned to scramble after his fallen blade. Already, another thick-necked

pirate was bundling towards Tom. Tom spun and kicked, driving the sole of his boot into the pirate's chest. The big man fell back with a grunt and Tom turned to scan the scene.

Elenna was scrambling through the window of the fallen coach. She leapt to the ground, her bow in her hands. *Thank goodness she's all right!*

"Kill the Avantian brats, you fools!" a harsh cry echoed from above. "Those runts will not foil my plans this time!" The voice sent a stab of hot rage through Tom's guts. He looked up, searching for Sanpao's scowling face.

Elenna lifted her bow and arrow skywards. At the same moment, a huge, bloated pirate swooped towards her through the air, hanging from the end of a lanyard.

"Watch out!" Tom cried. But Elenna was ready, swinging her bow like a club the moment the pirate's boots touched the ground. *SMACK!* Elenna's bow hit him over the temple, and he fell headlong into the sand.

Tom saw a blur of movement from the corner of his eye and turned to see another barrel-chested pirate swinging towards him. He threw up his shield and felt the impact jar his forearms as the pirate slammed into the wood, bouncing off and landing in a crouch. Tom lowered his shield and charged, driving his elbow hard into the man's gut. As the pirate staggered back, Tom brought his elbow up, catching the man's stubbled jaw with a crack. The pirate stumbled away from him, clutching his chin.

"Right!" Elenna cried, scowling up at Sanpao's ship. "I've had enough of your bragging and cursing." She lifted her bow and arrow, and fired. Her arrow soared upwards towards the flying ship, slicing through one of the lines for the mainsail with a *twang*. The two ends coiled away, and the sail started to flap wildly.

"Hold our course, you worthless snot-rags!" Sanpao cried to his crew. Elenna let another arrow fly, and another, severing more lines. The pirates aboard raced up the rigging, tugging at whipping ropes and flapping canvas, while those left on the ground stared upwards, open-mouthed. The ship was tipping and heaving in the sky as if it was being tossed on a stormy sea.

Sanpao leaned over the gunwale, his eyes burning with fury. "Don't go thinking you've won, you snivelling land-rat!" he shouted at Tom. "We've got a lot more fun and games in store. Once you've met our

next little challenge, you're going
to wish you'd never dragged your
worthless hide across the ocean!"
He turned back to his men as his
ship listed suddenly, before veering

sharply towards the eastern horizon.

Tom and Elenna turned to the pirates left behind on the beach.

"Are you ready for a second round?" Tom shouted. The brawny men glanced at each other, then at their retreating ship, before finally turning tail and lumbering away, kicking up puffs of sand as they went.

Elenna shrugged. "So much for loyalty," she said.

Tom shielded his eyes and glanced after Sanpao's flying ship. It was already little more than a dot in the shimmering sky.

"The only loyalty Sanpao knows is to himself," Tom said. "But he's made a mistake in coming here. If it's a fight he's after, I'm ready for him."

3

TROUBLE IN JENGTOR

We must get to Jengtor, Tom thought. *But how?* He scanned the empty road that swept around the coastline, then turned to gaze inland. Grassy fields studded with red and blue flowers stretched towards low hills in the distance. Bright butterflies flitted above

the gently swaying stems. Fury
boiled in Tom's belly at the thought
of Sanpao and his pirate crew
destroying the peace of this place.
*And if Sanpao's here, that means
Kensa won't be far behind with her
evil magic...*

"Tom!" Elenna said, pointing
up towards the hazy hills in the
distance. Tom followed the line of
her finger, and saw a dark blot in
the sky. He tightened his grip on his
sword. *Another pirate attack?* But
as the dark object approached, Tom
could see it was far too small to
be a ship. Soon he could make out
flapping wings.

"It's just a bird," he said. He

called on the enhanced vision from his magic helmet, and saw that the bird was small and plump, covered in turquoise feathers. As it flew directly overhead, it opened its beak and let a tiny glass vial fall. Tom grabbed Elenna's arm and tugged her backwards as the vial shattered where they had been standing, sending up a plume of swirling blue smoke. The smoke twisted into a column, quickly solidifying into the form of a figure – a dark-haired woman in a long blue cloak patterned with stars, and fastened with a brooch bearing the dragon crest of Gwildor.

"Please, don't flee, Tom and

Elenna," the woman said. Her face
was lined, her eyes troubled. "We
are glad to welcome two brave

young warriors to our kingdom. You come at our time of need. I am Irina, Witch to Emperor Jeng of Gwildor. I come to meet you in place of Freya, our Mistress of the Beasts. Jengtor is under attack."

"I feared as much!" Tom said, marvelling at the magic. "We have already met with Sanpao and his crew."

Irina dipped her head. "The Pirate King sailed his ship over Jengtor and sent a barrage of cannon fire towards the city. I was able to create a force field to deflect his attack, but Sanpao had another trick up his sleeve. He has poured a most curious potion onto my force field, and it is slowly eating away at the magical barrier."

"That must be Kensa's work," Tom said, balling his fists. "Sanpao doesn't have the brains to concoct such a potion."

Irina sighed. "I fear you are right. The force field is holding for now, but soon Kensa's potion will burn a hole big enough for the ship to pass through. And when that happens..." The witch's voice tailed off, her expression grave.

"Are you able to evacuate the city?" Elenna asked.

Irina shook her head. "Not while the force field is up. Nothing can get in, and nothing can get out. And if I were to remove the force field to let people get to safety, we'd be vulnerable to Sanpao's cannons."

"But surely Freya could summon the Good Beasts to defend the city?" Elenna said.

Irina dropped her eyes to her hands, clasped together against her robe.

Tom's stomach twisted with worry. "Is my mother all right?" he asked. But he already knew the answer. If Freya were all right, Irina wouldn't be with him now.

Irina met Tom's eyes, and the gentle kindness in her expression sent another spike of fear through his gut. "She is alive," the witch said. "And she's getting our very best care. But she is sick and delirious. We believe a spy from Sanpao's crew somehow managed to sneak into the kitchens of the Imperial Palace, to poison her food."

Tom felt a lurching dizziness. "Can I help her?" he asked.

Irina shook her head sadly. "The kingdom's best physicians are caring for her as we speak. We will let no further harm come to her. But she will not be able to summon the Good Beasts to our aid. Gwildor is alone in this battle – and many thousands of lives are at stake."

Tom put his hand on the hilt of his sword, fierce determination building inside him. "Gwildor is never alone," he said. "Elenna and I will not let Sanpao harm your city. And, while there is blood in my veins, that treacherous pirate will pay for his attack on my mother."

BEAST FROM THE DEEP

"You must reach Jengtor quickly," Irina said. "I fear we do not have long." She bowed her head, and the magical image faded, leaving Tom and Elenna alone.

Elenna shaded her eyes and gazed towards the soft swell of forested hills in the distance.

"Which way?" she asked.

Tom touched the yellow jewel in his shield and closed his eyes, concentrating on an image of the map of Gwildor. In his mind's eye, he found the spot where they had come ashore, then traced a path to Jengtor on the other side of the kingdom. He opened his eyes.

"Jengtor is near the western coast," Tom said. "Further than we have ever travelled in Gwildor before."

"In that case, we'd better find those horses," Elenna said.

A trail of hoof-prints led away from the fallen coach. Tom and Elenna followed the prints until they found the two grey mares cropping the grass at the edge of some dunes. Elenna rummaged in her pack and pulled out two dried apples. She handed one to Tom, and they both quietly approached the horses.

As they drew close, the horses' heads came up and turned, their soft eyes watching with interest. Tom held out his apple, and Elenna did the same.

"Angel?" Tom said gently, testing out the name as one of the animals approached him. Her ears pricked up in recognition and her long tail swished. *Good guess!* Tom thought. "Here you go, girl," he said, holding

the apple under her nose. Now that
the pirates were gone, the horse's
body seemed relaxed, and her huge
eyes were calm and curious. Tom
stroked her head as she nibbled
the apple. Elenna's horse, Star,
had taken her apple too, and was

munching on it contentedly. Elenna reached over the horse's head, and lifted away the heavy yoke that had attached her to the carriage.

Once both horses were free of their yokes and had finished their apples, Tom and Elenna swung up into the saddles.

"So, shall we head west?" Elenna asked.

"Not yet," Tom said. "I want to get a view of the terrain. There are a few different routes we can take on horseback, but there could be obstacles on the way. I don't know which will get us there fastest." Tom engaged the power of his golden helmet to gaze westward, but his view was blocked by the hills. He turned back to the coastline, and pointed to a lighthouse a little way to the south. "Let's head to the lighthouse," he told Elenna. "We'll get a better view of the kingdom from the top. Then we can decide which path to take."

Elenna nodded, and Tom tapped his heels to his horse's sides, starting off at a trot. Once they were back on the coastal path, he and Elenna kicked the horses into a gallop, and rode hard towards the lighthouse. The path was smooth and well trodden, and Tom relaxed into the rhythm of Angel's swift stride. Before long, they reached the end of the stone jetty that led out into the sea and pulled their horses to a halt. There was a tethering post near the jetty, and Tom and Elenna tied the horses up, leaving them each with another apple.

As they strode towards the lighthouse, waves slapped against the quay, sending up a spray that cooled Tom's face. Near to the beach, the water was crystal clear, but further from the shore, it darkened to a shadowy blue-green swell.

The lighthouse stretched far above them, its whitewashed walls blazing in the sun. At the top was a glass section surrounded by a

railing. A wooden door stood open
at the base of the tower. Tom poked
his head through to find a narrow
stone staircase spiralling tightly

around a central post. "Hello?" he called. His voice echoed hollowly back towards him. He and Elenna stepped inside and climbed. Their boots rang harshly on the stone, and the roar of the sea swirled around them.

I suppose the keeper probably only comes at night to set the fires, he thought.

It was a long way up, and by the time they reached the top, Tom felt hot and sticky under his clothes. The whole staircase smelled of old ashes, and at the top, shielded from the wind by the glass wall, they found the blackened wood from an old fire.

"Phew!" Tom said, stopping for a moment to get his breath before going out onto the balcony. Once outside, he turned away from the sea to study the lie of the land.

The deep, rich colours of Gwildor were spread out below him: lush grassland, cut through by snaking sapphire rivers and paths in vibrant reds and browns. To the south, Tom could see the thick, dense greenery of the Rainbow Jungle. He bit his lip, considering the route along the jungle's edge. It was full of dangers, but with the threat of a pirate attack from the sky it might still be safer than crossing the open grassland.

Behind him, Elenna gasped. "Oh no!" Tom turned to find her looking out over the jetty. He rushed to her side, expecting to see the horses bolting, or Sanpao's pirate ship returning.

Instead, he found a tall, slim figure with flame-red hair standing on the jetty, looking up at the balcony and smiling. Tom gritted his teeth, every muscle in his body clenching. *Kensa.* As the Evil Witch caught Tom's eye, her smile spread into a grin.

"Well, well, well!" she called, her husky voice raised to be heard over the waves. "It's so typical of you young heroes to go racing straight *towards* danger rather than away from it. Which I suppose is why all young heroes end up the same way – in agony! And since you've been kind enough to save me the trouble of actually looking for you, I shall reward you with a front-row view of my next move. Now watch!"

Kensa's hand moved as quickly as a snake. With one flourish, she pulled a dark vial from her cloak and uncorked it. Then she tipped the contents into the sea.

The Evil Witch let out a delighted laugh as an inky stain spread through the water, swirling on the current like smoke. She tossed the empty vial aside, before turning

and racing towards the shore, her
long cloak flaring behind her.

Beneath the tower, huge bubbles
rose from the blackened water. Tom
craned forwards, adrenaline pulsing
through his veins as he stared at the

dark, boiling water. Two huge black
eyes broke the surface, followed
by a pair of massive pincers. Long,
spindly legs scrabbled at the rock
of the jetty, dragging a broad,
armoured body out of the sea. The

creature that emerged was covered
in the dusky stain made by Kensa's
potion. Clumps of dark, straggly
weed trailed from its legs and
back, and its thick, jointed shell
was craggy and scarred, suggesting

great age. Its long body tapered to a
huge, fanned tail.

A lobster? Tom gaped at the vast,
blackened Beast. It was the size
of a whale. Its dark eyes swivelled
upwards on stubby stalks until they

came to rest on Tom. Its antennae twitched, sending an icy chill washing over him.

I'm its target, Tom thought.

A FALL INTO DARKNESS

The creature clambered over
the jetty towards the lighthouse,
feelers whipping from side to side
and pincers clashing together like
hungry jaws. Tom put his hand on
the red jewel in his belt, almost
staggering backwards when he felt
the Beast's boiling rage sweep over

him in a ferocious wave. He could hear the creature's voice in his mind – a rough, grating sound as powerful and inhuman as the roar of the sea.

I am Styro, and I am cursed to destroy, the Beast cried. *I will bring chaos to Gwildor!*

The creature reared upwards, a writhing dark wall of stained armour and matted weed. He drew back one mighty foreleg and sent his pincer smashing towards the lighthouse.

CRASH! Tom staggered back as the building shook. Beside him, Elenna grabbed the metal railing. Styro lifted his other claw. *SNAP!*

It clamped shut on the lighthouse,
sending chunks of stone clattering
down onto the jetty. Tom drew his
sword and held it high as the Beast

heaved himself upwards. *CRUNCH!*
Styro's pincer snapped shut once
more and the giant lobster pulled
himself higher. *He's climbing the
tower!*

"We have to get out of here!"
Elenna cried. Another thud echoed
around them, and the building
juddered, sending her careering
into the thick glass window. She
turned and started towards the
lighthouse staircase. Tom caught
her shoulder.

"What if the building collapses?"
he said. "It might be safer to jump."
But even as he said the words, he
knew it was too late. He could hear
the crunching, splintering crash of

Styro's pincers crushing the bricks of the tower as he climbed. The Beast's long antennae reached over the metal parapet, twitching and lashing towards him. "Get back!" Tom told Elenna, lifting his sword before them as they backed against the glass.

A vast claw clamped shut around the metal railing. Styro's murderous eyes appeared over the balcony. Elenna lifted her bow and took aim.

"No!" Tom cried. "We can't kill him. He's not evil – he's under a dark spell."

Elenna let her bow fall as the Beast's feelers groped towards them. Between the twitching, lashing feelers, two rows of vertical tooth-like structures chomped together. Tom's gut churned with fear. One of the lobster's claws was still clamped to the metal railing, but the other swooped through the air like a club. Tom leapt aside, tugging Elenna with him as the claw smashed against the parapet floor. It left a crack in the flagstones and shattered the glass with a crash. The Beast lifted his claw again, and Tom lunged forwards, swiping out with the flat of his sword.

Smash! Tom's sword thudded against the huge mandible, sending a shockwave along his arm. It was like hitting a wall.

Styro's open claw snapped towards him, deflecting Tom's sword and clamping around his waist.

"Aargh!" Tom gasped as the breath was squeezed from his lungs.

"Tom!" Elenna cried. She lifted her bow and smashed it down on the claw, but Styro only squeezed tighter. Tom's feet were yanked from the ground and his stomach lurched as Styro's massive claw plucked him from the balcony and flung him free.

Bright sun and blue sky swooped past as Tom spun in the air, then his view was replaced by the cobbles of the jetty rushing up to meet him. Tom's nerves jangled and his muscles clenched in panic. He scrabbled for his shield, tugging it from his back and twisting to hold it above his head, slowing his fall with the magic of Arcta's eagle feather.

But it was too late. He hit the jetty, his legs crumpling as he tumbled head over heels. His body screamed with pain in too many places to count.

Splash! Suddenly the sounds of shattering rock and scrabbling limbs were gone, replaced by eerie silence. Glittering ripples shone above him, and a warm weightless feeling bathed his aching limbs. He was cushioned in soft, golden light, tugged gently downwards by the current's embrace. The sunlight above him grew fainter. Shadows groped up towards him,

and somewhere in the back of his
dazed mind, he felt a stab of alarm.
His pulse was loud in his ears and
his lungs were throbbing, burning,
twitching for air.

I'm in the ocean, Tom thought. *I'm drowning!*

He shook himself, clearing his befuddled senses, and kicked hard with his legs. His shield

waterlogged clothes were
weighing him down. He kicked and
kicked, finally bursting through the
sparkling ripples of the surface.

He drew a deep breath and felt his dizziness subside. Then his heart jolted with terror. The lighthouse reached far above him, covered in dark gashes where the Beast's pincers had struck. On the jetty at the base of the structure, the massive, armoured bulk of Styro crouched, waiting. His dark, murderous gaze rested on Tom, his vast pincers gnashing together.

Then the Beast plunged into the waves.

A DARING RESCUE

Only Styro's black eyes and armoured back were visible above the surface as he tore through the ocean towards Tom. Tom reached for his sword, but realised he couldn't fight while treading water. He dived forwards, striking out at an angle towards the shore, but the Beast changed course to block his

path. He reared up before Tom –
knobbly black armour and skeletal
legs surrounded by stinking,
billowing weed. A huge black claw
sliced through the waves, just below
the surface.

"Ahhh!" Tom cried out in agony as
Styro's pincer snapped shut around
his ribs once more. He thrashed and
squirmed in the Beast's grip, trying
to force open the giant pincer – but
even with the magical strength
from his golden breastplate, it was
like trying to bend steel. The claw
tugged at his body, pulling him
downwards. Tom kicked his legs,
trying to free himself, but Styro
was too strong.

Just before he was pulled under, Tom angled his head back to take a gulp of air. He caught a glimpse of Elenna standing poised on the metal balcony that ran around the top of the lighthouse with her arms above her head and a single arrow clutched in her fist.

What is she doing? Tom wondered. *It looks like she's about to jump!*

Then the view was snatched away – bright daylight was replaced by a shadowy silence. Tom was swallowed down into the ocean, his ribs clamped tight in Styro's claw. He blinked in the dimness, and found himself looking straight into the Beast's bulbous eyes.

Jointed legs covered in sharp spines lashed towards him. Tom tried to bat them away with his sword – but underwater, his movements were slow and clumsy, like in a nightmare. The pain in his ribs was tremendous and his bruised lungs were shuddering for air. He was powerless.

One of Styro's legs lashed across his face and he almost gasped with the pain, but somehow managed to clench his teeth against the deadly urge. If he opened his mouth, it would fill with water – and he would be dead in seconds.

Suddenly, a cloud of bubbles erupted nearby. Elenna was in

the water with him, swimming
as swiftly and sleekly as a seal.
She jumped! Tom realised in
amazement. *She dived right from
the very top of the lighthouse!*

Styro's black eyes swivelled
towards her, and his heavy claw
whipped out, but Elenna kicked her
legs, ducked beneath it and swam
on. Tom's pulse was thudding in his
ears as his friend swooped towards
him. His whole body was screaming
for air. Elenna drew back her arm,
then drove it forwards, sending her
arrow straight into the armoured
claw that was crushing Tom's chest.
The claw shuddered and Tom felt
the hideous pain in his chest relax.

He was free! But then the water
around him erupted in a flurry
of bubbles and flailing armoured
limbs.

The Beast writhed wildly, his
claws opening and shutting and its

antennae whipping about. Tom's head felt like it might burst from the pressure. His body was weak with lack of air and he didn't know if he had the strength to swim to the surface. He felt Elenna grab his hand and tug, dragging him upwards through the water. His best friend's bravery sent a surge through Tom, and he found new energy to kick his legs and swim.

Finally they burst out into the sunlight. Tom gasped, his first breath flooding through his body like a powerful healing potion. Elenna climbed onto the jetty and held out a hand. Tom gripped it and clambered out, clutching his side

as he collapsed onto the wet stone.
He lifted his sodden tunic and saw
a long bloody gash surrounded by
deep purple bruising. It looked bad,
but wasn't deadly. He took a deep
breath, steeling himself.

*The pain is just going to have
to wait.*

He glanced out to sea. The giant
lobster was watching them. As soon
as his dark eyes locked with Tom's,
he launched himself forwards.

"Run!" Elenna cried, dashing
away towards the shore. Tom turned
and raced after her, clutching his
ribs, every step sending a stabbing
pain through his chest. He felt the
jetty shudder beneath his feet,

then heard a scrabble of pincers on stone. He glanced back to see Styro clambering onto the jetty. The dripping weed that covered his body trailed over the stone as he chased them.

As soon as Tom and Elenna were clear of the sea, they leapt from the jetty onto wet sand. A moment later, Styro clattered down after them. Tom scanned the beach as they ran on, looking for anything that might give them an advantage over the Beast. The golden sands gave way to grassland to the south. To the north the beach was bounded by craggy cliffs. Tom spotted a row of deep shadows along the base of the rock face, and felt a flicker of hope. He pointed.

"Head for those caves!" he called to Elenna. "Maybe if we trap Styro inside, he won't have space to fight back!"

Elenna nodded and set off. Tom followed her, quickly finding himself gasping for breath, winded by the grinding pain of ribs he suspected might have been broken. Only calling on the power of his golden leg armour allowed him to keep pace with Elenna. Behind him, the eerie scrabble of Styro's legs was getting closer by the moment. He glanced over his shoulder to see the vast lobster dragging himself

along behind them, an ugly blot
of darkness against the sapphire
sky. The creature's mighty claws
clashed together as it moved, and
its spindly limbs creaked like dead
wood in a storm. Styro was so close
Tom could smell the pungent stink
of the weed that covered his body.
He could hear the slithering sound
of the long strands slipping over
the sand.

Tom and Elenna pounded
onwards into the shadow of the
cliff and ducked into the nearest
cave. Inside, Tom found himself
in half-darkness, surrounded by
the echoing roar of the sea. Once
his eyes had adjusted, he saw that

the cave was bigger than he had
expected, with high, craggy walls,
dripping with slime.

Elenna stood with her hands on
her knees, catching her breath. "So
what's the plan?" she asked.

"Watch the entrance," Tom told her. "I'm going to fix my ribs so I can fight the Beast at full strength. Then we'll lure him in here, and defeat him."

Elenna nodded, and crossed to the cave mouth. She leaned her back against the rock and peered out at the beach, her one remaining arrow raised like a dagger. Tom took the green jewel from his belt and held it against his ribs. He focussed his mind, directing the jewel's healing magic to the source of his pain. His ribs began clicking back into place, and he started to breathe more easily. But before he had re-set them all, Elenna was leaping back

from the cave entrance, her arrow
ready.

"Styro's coming now!" she hissed.
A vast, dark form blocked the cave
mouth, plunging them into darkness.
Tom gritted his teeth in frustration
and placed his green jewel back in
his belt. Each breath sent a stabbing
pain through his chest, but he stood
tall and gripped the hilt of his
sword, ready to face the Beast.

THE TURN OF THE TIDE

Tom stood with his sword and shield raised, straining his eyes into the darkness. At his side, Elenna had her arrow drawn back, ready to fire. A terrible smell, like rotting fish and seaweed baking in the midday sun, wafted towards them in waves.

As Tom's eyes adjusted, he saw
Styro's pincers reaching into
the cave, followed by his broad,
armoured head. Tom squared
his shoulders and tightened his
grip on his sword. The Beast's
shell seemed to radiate gloom,
swallowing what little light there
was. But his bulbous eyes shone
with a menacing light of their own.
The acrid fumes from Styro's shell
caught in Tom's throat, making him
cough and gag. He blinked to clear
his streaming eyes, bringing the
swimming shadows back into focus.

A giant claw loomed out of the
darkness. Tom spun and lunged,
putting the full weight of his body

behind his sword. He smashed the
claw aside, but then stumbled and
almost fell, the cave seeming to

twist sickeningly around him. As he scrambled back to Elenna's side, he found she was blinking hard, as if she was dizzy too. *The fumes from the weed on Styro's back must be toxic,* Tom realised. *We have to get out!* Tom's muddled senses registered a giant black shape crashing down from above. He leapt back and swung his sword.

But Styro's massive claw flicked it aside with such power, Tom thought his arm might have been ripped off. The blow sent him staggering backwards further into the cave. Elenna lunged past him, stabbing at Styro's other pincer with the head of her arrow, but the claw snapped towards her. She reared back out of reach of the Beast, her footsteps slow and sluggish.

Tom and Elenna stood side by side, their breath coming in wheezing gasps. The shadows seemed to spin before Tom's eyes and the ground lurched. He could hardly focus.

"We'll have to make a run for it!" Tom said.

At the same moment, Styro's open pincer swung towards him.

Tom threw himself under the claw and rolled between the creature's skeletal legs, coming to rest under the Beast's armoured belly. Straggly weed hung thick all around him.

"Go!" he shouted to Elenna, gasping as choking bile rose in his throat. Red spots swam before his eyes. He turned his head to take a breath, gathering his strength before scrambling towards the dazzling light of the cave mouth.

The light vanished as Tom was smashed violently to the ground, pinned by the monster's fanned tail. He lay for a moment, gasping, sickness churning inside him, a taste of metal filling his mouth. Suddenly he felt warm water sweep around him, tugging the sand from under his body, before sliding away. *The tide is coming in!*

Tom heard a loud, echoing thud

and a panicked yelp from deep inside the cave. *Elenna's still trapped!*

He called on all his strength, swallowed his sickness and bucked, driving his shoulders up against Styro's tail. A shudder ran through the fanned armour plates, and the tail jerked upwards. Tom rolled away and scrambled to his feet. Then he turned and leapt onto the Beast's weed-covered back. Styro reared, screeching with rage. Tom plunged his hands into the stinking weed and clung tight as the furious lobster writhed, trying to shake him free. From the corner of his eye, he saw Elenna race past the

Beast, out towards the sunlight.
Relief powered through his veins,
giving him strength. *She's free!* He
turned, bent his knees, and kicked
off the Beast's shell, leaping after
his friend.

As he flew from Styro's back towards the sunlight, Tom's guts clenched in horror. Styro's flat slab of a tail flicked sideways, slamming into Elenna as she passed and throwing her into the shallows. She lay motionless, her face hidden beneath the waves. Tom hit the ground running and splashed through the water, falling to his knees beside her. He lifted her head and shoulders above the incoming tide.

Behind him, he could hear the clamour of the Beast backing his colossal body out of the cave.

"Elenna? Are you all right?" Tom cried.

Elenna's eyes flickered open and she coughed. Seawater flowed from her mouth and nose, and she started to struggle, her arms flailing and her eyes wide with panic.

"Elenna! Stop it, I've got you!"

Tom said, holding tight to her arm.

Her panicked eyes met his. "What's going on?" she asked hoarsely.

"You were knocked out," Tom told her. "You almost drowned. Can you make it back to the beach?"

Elenna glanced towards the narrow strip of sand that was left to the west, and nodded. Tom pulled her to her feet, relief flooding through him as she half ran, half staggered away. Then he turned towards the Beast.

The giant lobster had emerged from the darkness. He lumbered around to face Tom, black weed billowing around him in the shallow waves, and his eyes glinting with spite.

Tom hunkered down, his sword and shield before him. He glanced up the beach. Elenna was stumbling out of the waves onto the sand. Beyond her, Tom could just make out Angel and Star, scuffing the ground at the shoreward end of the jetty. At the other end of the structure, surrounded by pounding waves, stood the battered and broken lighthouse. Great cracks and gashes in the stone showed where Styro had attacked it.

One more blow from Styro's claw is all it would take... Tom thought, a plan taking shape in his mind.

He put his hand to the red jewel
in his belt and locked eyes with
the furious Beast. "What are you
waiting for?" he called.

I told you to run, puny child! the Beast cried. *I will crush your soft body to pulp!*

Tom could feel the rage radiating from the creature – the desperate need to destroy. With a screech like a thousand nails scraping on glass, Styro lowered his head and charged towards Tom.

LIGHT DEFEATS
THE DARK

Tom called on the power of his
golden boots and leapt away across
the beach, fighting through knee-
deep water. The current sent waves
smashing against his legs. The
beach was almost gone now, and
foaming breakers crashed against
the jetty. Tom glanced back to see

Styro lurching after him, moving quickly despite the sodden weed clinging to his shell.

The Beast is taking the bait, he thought. *I just hope this works!* He raced on towards to the jetty, plunging through water, forcing his legs to move against the tide. He kept his eyes focussed on the lighthouse ahead. Finally he reached the jetty, and leapt. He caught hold of the edge of the causeway, hauled himself up, and turned. The Beast was just behind him now, ploughing through the rising waves, a white V of foam in its wake.

Tom dashed towards the

lighthouse. He could hear the clack and clatter of giant lobster feet scrambling onto the cobbles behind him. Once he reached the shadow of the stone tower, he turned and stood tall.

The Beast was before him, eight legs spread wide over the stones, vast armoured body hanging above them. His pincers clashed together, and his bulbous eyes burned with rage. Tom reached again for his red jewel.

"Styro!" he called. "I don't want to hurt you. You must fight the evil enchantment Kensa placed on you. She is using you as her slave!"

The giant lobster lifted his head

and let out a screech so loud that Tom clapped his hands over his ears. His eyes flashing with wild rage, Styro lowered his massive head and charged.

Tom stood poised on the balls of his feet, waiting for the right moment. The Beast's massive claws swung through the air, snapping towards him. Tom gritted his teeth, bent his legs and sprang.

He threw himself up and forwards through the air, dipping his head and reaching his arms downwards towards the creature. He landed on his hands on Styro's knobbly shell, and used his arms to launch himself upwards again, flipping over the

lobster's back, and landing on his feet on the jetty beyond.

Tom turned and watched Styro plough onwards like a giant battering ram and crash headfirst into the lighthouse. He felt the impact through the stone beneath his feet. Styro's head was embedded in the base of the lighthouse. His legs scrabbled at the ground as he tried to tug himself free, but his efforts sent more chunks of stone raining downwards onto his back from above. Tom could see the cracks in the lighthouse

wall gaping wider, the top section
starting to lean. He held his breath,
frozen to the spot, as the huge mass
of stone toppled through the air…

SMASH! The lighthouse crashed
down onto Styro's thrashing body,
burying the Beast completely. Dust
billowed upwards, mingled with the

spray of the sea. A terrible screech of pain and rage pierced through the thunder of falling rubble.

Tom watched, his muscles tensed, as the clatter of falling masonry subsided. A mound of broken stone lay at the end of the jetty where the lighthouse had once stood. Nothing moved except the pounding waves. Tom put a hand to the red jewel, searching for any sign of life in the Beast. At first he could feel nothing. Then he sensed a flicker of movement. He grabbed for his sword, but then relaxed his grip. There was nothing Beastly about the gentle, bewildered presence he sensed awakening beneath the stone. Whatever lay under the rubble was no longer in the thrall of Kensa's poison.

Tom let out a long, relieved sigh and strode towards the pile of rubble. He dug with his hands, letting bricks clatter away over the jetty into the sea. He held his breath as he tugged at stinking tendrils of weed, lifting handfuls of the matted stuff away. Finally, he saw a patch of pale shell, iridescent in the sun. He shoved more rubble and weed aside, and a small, pearl-grey lobster crawled out into the light, free of weed. His eyes swivelled briefly to meet Tom's – then he scuttled over the fallen debris, slid into the waves, and was gone.

As Tom pushed himself to his feet, the world around him lurched into a spin. He closed his eyes to stop himself sinking back to his knees and blinked the dizziness away. He looked again at the dark weed strewn about his feet. *That's powerful stuff*, he thought. *It might prove useful on a future Quest.* He pulled away a clump of the stinking tendrils and walked back up the jetty, holding the weed as far from his face as he could. The sea was starting to lap over the causeway now, and the wet cobbles shone gold in the sun. At the far end of

the jetty, Elenna was making her
way slowly towards the horses.
The rest of the shoreline and the
grassland beyond were deserted.
*Kensa was too cowardly to stay
and watch me break her spell!* Tom

thought. *No surprises there!*

The dappled mares were tramping at the ground, their ears twitching and their eyes rolling nervously towards the sea on either side. Tom patted Angel's flank, and shoved the putrid weed deep into her leather saddlebag.

Elenna was leaning on Star, clutching her head, and grimacing as if the sun hurt her eyes. "What happened?" she asked, blinking hard and peering at Tom. Her eyes were bloodshot and her face was grey.

Tom took Epos's talon from his shield. He held it to Elenna's head, and saw her eyes shift back into focus. Elenna let out a grateful sigh and the colour returned to her cheeks. "Thank you!" she said. "I felt like my head was splitting in half."

"Styro is free," Tom told her, taking the green jewel from his belt to finish repairing his broken ribs. "But we've lost precious time. We need to get to Jengtor, and fast." Tom vaulted up onto Angel's back. "If Kensa's potions are powerful enough to turn ordinary creatures into Beasts…" Tom stopped, his throat suddenly tight as he thought of his mother – sick, besieged by pirates, and still a long ride away. He swallowed and forced himself to breathe deeply. Fear wouldn't help Freya. Elenna looked up at him, her eyes fierce with determination.

"Irina is looking after Freya," she said. "We've defeated Kensa's Beast. We'll get to Jengtor before it's too late and we'll defeat Sanpao as well." She leapt up onto Star's back and grabbed the reins.

"You're right," Tom said firmly, turning his eyes towards the Rainbow Jungle. "While there is blood in my veins, I will find a way to cure my mother, and I will drive Kensa and Sanpao out of Gwildor for good!"

1

CONGRATULATIONS, YOU HAVE COMPLETED THIS QUEST!

At the end of each chapter you were awarded a special gold coin.
The QUEST in this book was worth an amazing 8 coins.

Look at the Beast Quest totem picture inside the back cover of this book to see how far you've come in your journey to become

MASTER OF THE BEASTS.

The more books you read, the more coins you will collect!

Do you want your own
Beast Quest Totem?
1. Cut out and collect the coin below
2. Go to the Beast Quest website
3. Download and print out your totem
4. Add your coin to the totem
www.beastquest.co.uk/totem

Don't miss the next exciting Beast Quest book, RONAK THE TOXIC TERROR!

Read on for a sneak peek...

CHAPTER ONE

THE BROKEN VIAL

Tom clung on tight to Angel's reins as they thundered along the rocky path. The horse was panting, but there was no time to stop and rest.

If they delayed now, they would be putting all of Gwildor in mortal danger.

The path dipped and rose again through long swaying grasses on either side. Tom threw a quick glance over his shoulder to check that Elenna was with him. His friend was crouched low over her own horse, Star. Her hair was streaming in the breeze, and her features were set with determination. Every now and again, her eyes flicked up towards the sky.

Tom knew exactly what she was looking for. At any minute, Sanpao's flying pirate ship might come swooping down from the sky and put a stop to their Quest. Tom followed his friend's gaze, and his heart lurched as he saw a dark shape flitting high above.

Phew! It was only a seagull.

Sanpao's probably too busy laying siege to Jengtor, making its innocent citizens suffer for the sake of his own greed...

Tom turned his attention back to the path ahead. *We have to get to Jengtor – and fast.* He couldn't stop thinking of his mother, trapped there in the capital of Gwildor, her body racked with poison from the evil magic of Kensa.

The rocky path veered off to the right, but Tom and Elenna kept heading straight inland. The sun sank lower in the sky, and when they reached the top of a hill, Elenna reined in her horse and let out a gasp. Below, farmland stretched out to the horizon. But the dazzling golden crops of Gwildor were faded and wilted to muddy browns and greens.

"What happened here?" muttered Elenna.

"I don't know," said Tom. "But I have a feeling I know who's responsible..."

Elenna nodded grimly. "Kensa," she said.

"Don't worry," Tom told her. "We won't let her get away with it."

They rode down the hillside. Up close, Tom saw that the crops had all wasted away. In some places they had rotted into a murky slime that smelled so bad that Tom and Elenna had to cover their noses with their sleeves.

Angel let out a whinny and slowed to a canter. The next moment Star reared up, almost throwing Elenna from his back. "Whoa there!" she cried.

Even the horses can tell that something's wrong.

"We'd better stop," said Elenna, stroking Star's neck to calm him. "We won't reach Jengtor before dusk, and the horses need a rest."

Tom glanced up at the sun, which was turning orange and sinking closer to the horizon. He knew his friend was right. He scanned around and spotted a shallow watering hole in the next field.

"Look!" he said, pointing. "We can camp there for the night, then set off at first light."

Tom's stomach squirmed as they approached the pool. The foul stench in the air got worse the closer they came.

"Poor creature," murmured Elenna, and Tom turned to see a cow lying dead on its side, its eyes shut and its belly swollen. There were others corpses further off.

Tom wished he could heal the animals with the power of the green jewel, but it was obvious that there was nothing he could do for them, even with magic.

Elenna shivered. "Something terrible happened here," she said quietly. "Maybe we shouldn't stay after all."

Tom brought Angel to a halt and dismounted. He crossed to the shallow pool of water and saw that it was thick, murky and green. There was no way they could drink it.

As he stepped back something crunched beneath his foot. Tom bent down and found shattered fragments of glass trodden into the mud.

A broken vial...

At once the sick feeling in his
stomach grew ten times worse.
The pieces of the vial looked
very familiar indeed. He turned to
Elenna, holding up the fragments for
her to see.

Elenna went pale. "It looks just like the one with that horrible magic potion inside, that Kensa used to conjure up Styro," she said.

"I'm afraid so," said Tom. "And if the potion could turn an ordinary lobster into a deadly lobster Beast…"

"What kind of Beast has Kensa created this time?" Elenna finished for him.

The air seemed to have turned suddenly chilly.

"We'll have to investigate," said Tom. "With my mother sick, there are no Good Beasts to protect Gwildor, so it's up to us to…" He trailed off as he saw something. A short distance away, there were hoofprints in the mud.

Giant hoofprints, far bigger than any horse's, and cloven like a goat's.

Elenna gasped, and looked at him. Tom knew she was thinking the same thing as he was. *Could those belong to the Beast?*

Read *Ronak The Toxic Terror* to find out what happens next!

FIGHT THE BEASTS,
FEAR THE MAGIC

Discover the new Beast Quest mobile game from

Available free on iOS and Android

  amazon.com

Guide Tom on his Quest to free the Good Beasts
of Avantia from Malvel's evil spells.

Battle the Beasts, defeat the minions,
unearth the secrets and collect
rewards as you journey through the
Kingdom of Avantia.

DOWNLOAD THE APP TO BEGIN
THE ADVENTURE NOW!